Faye Starling

Blood Red Wood

novum ▲ pro

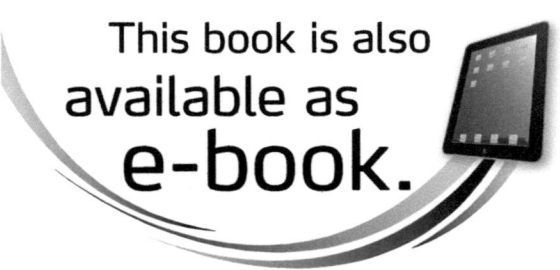

This book is also available as e-book.

www.novum-publishing.co.uk

© 2021 novum publishing

ISBN 978-3-99107-602-5
Editing: Hugo Chandler, BA
Cover photos: Dolores Preciado, LIAO QIONGNA, Casanowe | Dreamstime.com
Cover design, layout & typesetting: novum publishing

www.novum-publishing.co.uk

To those who encouraged me, believed in me.

Natasha at the age of 5, with her Romanian parents had come to live in Edinburgh, Scotland. In 1964 Romania after Stalin's death, declared autonomy within the Communist Bloc. Free movement for Romanian people was granted for those who wished to move from their homeland. Natasha's father, an academic, applied and was offered a job at the University in Edinburgh to lecture on European History. Her Mother, Alina had been happy to move from Rumania, she adored and admired her husband, and she knew that whatever decision he might make would be for the wellbeing of her and their daughter, Natasha.

Natasha as a chubby child grew to be slim. At eighteen she was five foot seven inches with beautiful auburn hair and dark blue eyes, which mirrored those of her father. After finishing university, she trained to be a Physiotherapist. There was a hint of her Slavic origin in her speech, mixed with a Scottish accent. The mix was charming.

★★★

David, born in Edinburgh, now at the age of thirty, had had several short-term relationships with women, during the eleven years it had taken him to become a doctor. Those he had found, he had not felt he could spend the rest of his life with, as none had ticked his imaginary boxes. None of them was the woman of his dreams. David was six foot two inches tall and well built. He liked to work out when he had the chance. His blonde hair was cut short. He had odd eyes, one was blue, the other green.

His father, Andrew had worked all his life as a self-employed painter and decorator, his own father had taught and shown him the skill. Due to his obvious ability, he was always recommended to other people, so he had rarely been out of work. His mother Margaret, until David had gone to university had been happy to be a housewife. Through a friend she was later offered a job in the local Fish and Chip shop. She was an excellent cook and had the type of character that people warmed to. Andrew had encouraged her to take the job if she wanted to.

★★★

Natasha was a shy person. She had had a few boyfriends who she dated as she grew up. The normal scenario as a young person changed from a child into maturity. She held her mother's advice close, which had been to find the man you love and do not let him go, when you find him. She wanted the kind of relationship, her parents had, so she was prepared to wait to find it.

★★★

Having only joined the Finnely Practice eight months previously David was concentrating on doing the work he enjoyed, focused on his chosen profession. He went to have lunch with his parents at the weekend, in their terraced home. Enjoying his parents company gave him time to relax. It also stopped him from thinking about the care of the patients who had visited throughout the week. His father told him about his current work. His Mother always asked jokingly, 'Have you found her yet?' because she knew how hard he worked. She tried to tell him that there was more to life than just work. His thoughts were mostly far from finding 'the one'.

★★★

When she was twenty-six years old Natasha met David. He was one of the General Practitioners within the surgery where she had recently found new work, attending twice a week. She liked and admired David's demeanour with patients who were referred to her. He had a way of making them feel as if their health problems had been listened to carefully, and that their care was uppermost in his mind.

8

If love at first sight was a possibility, it happened. One look at Natasha was enough. When she was on duty, David found it difficult to keep his eyes off her, although they were both in their work environment. At night in bed alone, David developed his plan of courtship, an old-fashioned term, as to what to do regarding Natasha. His mind was set on starting a relationship with her somehow. The next time they met he plucked up the courage to ask her out for a drink that evening. Natasha without even considering the implications, agreed. They met in the nearest local pub. Hours passed as they told each other their respective histories. They laughed and without holding back they discussed their individual aims for the future.

Returning to his flat David could not get Natasha out of his mind, her gorgeous auburn hair cut into a stylish bob, her smile and her sparkling blue eyes. Natasha sat with a warm cup of coffee on her settee and thought about David's odd, coloured eyes, the way he made her laugh, how special he had made her feel, listening intently to her every word, unlike with the other boyfriends she had had previously, Cupid had struck hard.

Within two months they decided to move in together. David's flat was small, with a kitchen, one bedroom a bathroom and a lounge; the windows of which looked over a lovely starlight view at night. Natasha arrived carrying two suitcases. David had emptied drawers and made space for her to put her belongings into. Their relationship developed without a hitch, with both sets of parents having been introduced and as they witnessed the undeniable love between them, they were happy that they had found each other.

★★★

After their first year together, very settled into the relationship they had formed, they decided to look for a holiday that they would both enjoy. David suggested going to visit Yosemite National Park in California, USA. Neither had visited the 'States' before.

Natasha agreed, looking forward to their first adventure as a couple. Arriving at Los Angeles Airport they picked up their rental car and drove towards San Francisco, along the Pacific Coast Highway, an incredibly beautiful road trip, the Pacific Ocean crashing against the cliffs as they drove above them. They stopped overnight at a Motel 6 and spent a day enjoying the sights, in San Francisco, visiting Fisherman's Wharf, and eating wonderful fresh seafood. They headed inland and arrived at Yosemite as dusk was falling, having stopped to buy drink, food and charcoal for the BBQ.

Their budget was limited. They could not afford to stay in one of the plush lodges. Instead, they had opted to take a tent in the tented village, which was on the edge of a tributary of the Merced River which ran through Yosemite. Hiking trails were also close, giving access to various incredible beauty spots which they hoped to discover. They were happy with their choice.

Excitement welled as David parked their car in the car park above the tented village. Having checked in, they carried food, drink, extras, small bags containing clothing and other essentials to tent, number 39. As they expected it was basic with bedding, towels, a bed, small cupboards plus a fridge which made up their holiday home. Outside was a wooden table with benches on both sides, plus standard BBQ facilities next to it. A thirty second walk to the amenities provided toilets and showers. They had decided that this would suit them and on arrival it was satisfactory.

They quickly unpacked everything. David began to fire up the BBQ. Natasha could not help kissing him as he prepared food for them. After eating American style hot dogs, in large, long buns, followed by fresh fruit, they sat at the table with a glass of wine, relaxing. They were both tired, it had been a long day, but they wanted to watch others around them doing similar things, kids enjoying the freedom in the almost wild place. It delighted them, talking quietly, as they observed those around them, preparing food for their families. Listening to the lulls in the conversation swirling around them, interrupted by people laughing, sometimes chatting loudly, and the odd tired child throwing a little tantrum, not wishing to be put to bed by an insistent father or mother. Most people greeted them as they walked by, or waved.

★★★

As night descended, the sun had disappeared, leaving amber and violet behind, people disappeared slowly into their tents. Natasha brushed her hand through David's thick blonde hair, kissed him and said, 'Come on, we don't have all that long here, we should go and see what is right on our doorstep.' Tiredness had left her, and she wanted to be with her man in a different setting. 'It's a fabulous night, warm with a halfmoon sitting in an inky coloured sky containing misty far-off planets' she said, 'Let's go and explore'.

Grabbing David by the arm, she pulled him up and they walked past those around them. Mothers having settled their children down to sleep, sat with a beer or a glass of wine on the benches, having hushed conversations with their husbands or partners. The odd man stood outside alone, drinking his last can of beer. Natasha was pleased to find happiness and contentment all around her. They found a path and followed it.

As they walked out of the tented area, leaving the people behind them, there was a small fir forest ahead. Following the path, David stopped. He was being cautious.

Natasha said tugging at his hand, 'Come on, I can hear a river'. They walked amongst the trees and arrived at a small grassy meadow. The river lay ahead, strong water rushing by; its sound quite forceful and musical.

Natasha could not keep the smile off her face as she stood beside the man she loved. The beauty of where they stood and the ambiance around her was almost a dream. She giggled and felt a little tipsy. Aware of the happiness on Natasha's face, David asked her whether she would like to have a child in the future, a subject they had not approached before?

Looking up at what seemed endless darkness pitted with bright stars, she thought about holding a baby in her arms, how that would feel? She whispered, 'Yes'.

They were totally alone, it was late. 'Lie down Tash and look at the stars,' David said in a hushed voice.

'I have never seen so many stars,' whispered Natasha, snuggling up to David on the grass.

'You are my star,' David replied.

He gently removed her jeans, he wanted her at that moment. He made love to her. It was raunchy, he had to control his need to own her completely. He felt it was necessary to make sure that she understood the depth of his love as he could not put it into words. He could not imagine life without her.

Natasha's body responded immediately to both their needs as she listened to the river running just in front of them. She glimpsed the stars above reaching infinity above her, felt the hot breath of her man on her cheek. She gripped him tightly as he brought her to her climax, that sweet moment when one becomes two. He heard Natasha when she moaned mutedly. That was his signal, he allowed himself to follow her. Watching her ride her own wave gave him so much excitement, looking deep into her blue eyes with starlight dancing in them. In that meadow they had found hidden depths in each other that they had never experienced before.

Walking with David's arm around her; totally in step, they arrived back at tent 39. They sat with a last glass of wine, quietly laughing, kissing and discussing their future. Both had confirmed further commitment to each other at an unexpected time, in a special place. Courage had come to them. This was the place they would never forget, as both felt inwardly that there was nothing that could part them, that they would stand side by side and deal with whatever life threw at them.

★★★

David woke early. He was extremely happy. He threw on the nearest clothes he could lay his hands on, he wanted to revisit the place they had been the night before. He wanted to go back and place it firmly in his memory. Natasha was still asleep. Leaving their tent nobody moved outside, so he quietly walked to the forest area. Dew dropped off the tall fir trees. The sky was a colour he could not describe; putty coloured. The stars had disappeared, and the sun had not yet appeared. Arriving at the meadow in the chill of the morning made him shiver a little. The meadow looked different in the half daylight. At the end of the path, he stopped. In front of him was a child with shaggy blond hair, wearing blue shorts, a red T shirt and barefoot. David judged roughly that he was about seven years old.

The child stood in the middle of the small meadow, staring at a young deer at the edge of the riverbank. The deer was looking at the boy. Neither of them moved. Minutes slipped by, then the early morning sun broke through and bathed the expanse in gold between them. It broke the spell which had kept them both immovable. The deer bolted, and the child watched it go. He turned around to see David standing there.

'She is always here at this time of day,' the child spoke with wisdom far beyond his age, as he walked past David and went up the path back to the tented village.

★★★

The smell of bacon woke Natasha.

'Come on sleepyhead, breakfast is nearly ready, I have a story to tell you.'

Natasha stretched, smiled and ran her figures through her tangled hair, finding several pieces of grass from the night before, which made her smile even more. She took a few seconds to feel the evidence of the night's passionate lovemaking in the meadow, then she grabbed her wash bag and went to have a quick shower.

When she arrived back, a feast was set before her, coffee made in a pan, fried bread, crispy bacon, and a fried egg that was plonked on her plate as she sat down. Suddenly she was ravenous and tucked in immediately.

David sat down beside her, smacked a kiss on her cheek and said with a big grin on his face, 'Good morning star of my life.'

'Morning lover,' she replied giggling. 'What story?'

'I slept very well,' David replied. 'But I woke early, just as dawn was breaking, you were sleeping peacefully, nothing was moving, so I decided to walk to where we were last night. As I came to the edge of the forest, in the meadow there was a small boy and a deer by the riverbank, looking at each other, neither moving. It was like a picture had been painted. Intrigued I stood back, and I waited to see what would happen next.

Minutes passed, as if the boy and the deer were the only things on earth. Me being the onlooker, I held my breath. The sun came out and broke their link, and the deer ran off into the forest. The young boy turned around, and walked past me muttering, 'She

14

is always there'. I have looked the deer species up. The deer here are Mule Deer, we may see some today.'

'What an experience!' Natasha replied. 'I wish I had been there.'

David watched the early morning sun splashing over Natasha's lovely auburn hair, flecked by bronze, and he thought how lucky he was, again.

★★★

After clearing their breakfast dishes, they sat together to plan the day. Looking at the National Park map for the best features to view during their short time, they tried to choose carefully. They did not want to use the car; they were prepared to hike to each beauty spot. Both were fit enough. Map in front of them on the table they did not notice the two young women in the tent opposite them, as they were immersed in their plans.

Two mugs of strong coffee were placed in front of them by Sophie who introduced herself. She was tall and lithe. Her long hair was blonde, worn in a ponytail, she had a lovely smile on her face. Her eyes were light grey. She was dressed in small cut off denim shorts, which accentuated the length of her legs, a khaki-coloured T-shirt with a small smiley face on it, and tan coloured trainers.

'For the next few days, we live in the tent opposite you. My friend here is called Ava,' she said gesturing towards Ava.

Thanking Sophie, they looked at Ava and greeted her. Ava was shortish, with a strong looking build. She had short brown hair and deep dull brown eyes, shadowed by thick bushy eyebrows. She lifted a limp hand up and waved it. Ava was dressed in black from head to foot. The women were obviously American.

15

Sophie glanced down at the map that David and Natasha were studying. She said, 'Ava is a fitness freak, we were thinking of going to Angel Falls. I have been told it is spectacular, would you like to join us?'

From the opposite side of the table Ava said offhandedly, 'We always walk to see sights, get exercise, do you like to do that?'

Natasha replied, 'We have not decided yet, but thank you for the offer of your company.'

★★★

Sophie and Ava made their breakfast and drank their coffee leisurely. They watched David and Natasha as they thought about going to Angel Falls, listening to their quiet talk, believing that they could not be overheard. The seed had been planted.

Sophie went to collect the coffee mugs she had given to them and asked nonchalantly, 'Have you decided to go to the falls? If so, do join us, the more the merrier.' Standing over them, Sophie smiled sweetly.

Natasha looked uncertainly towards David. Her eyebrow went up as a question mark. She had not planned to spend the day with outsiders. David thought the women seemed pleasant enough, willing to walk to an attraction that both parties wished to view.

'Why not?' Ava asked, appearing relaxed on the opposite bench. 'We can make food to take for all of us. Sophie is an expert sandwich maker. All you will need to do is to bring water.'

'No, we must help,' Natasha replied instinctively.

'Forget it,' Sophie said. Her smile had not diminished, cutting short any negative reply. 'Done deal,' she said turning her back on them to go and clear their own breakfast table. 'See you in half an hour,' she said over her shoulder.

***

Dwayne wandering through the tented village, he was a day visitor, caught the last words spoken between the two parties. He said to David, 'I could not help overhearing, sorry to interrupt, are you going to Angel Falls?' David nodded. 'I am a photographer, and I was planning to go there myself today. Can I join your group as it is always nice to have company on an expedition, I think?'

Natasha looked at him and thought that out of the bunch, Sophie and Ava included, he appeared a more natural, trustworthy person; somebody who she didn't have to worry about. He was a little chubby, not much taller than herself, with spiky black hair and a round face. She could not distinguish the colour of his eyes. However, they appeared to be a deep brown, almost plum. He wore light brown knee length shorts, a T-shirt in the same colour and sturdy brown walking boots. He had an expensive looking camara slung over his shoulder, with a large telescopic lens attached.

David asked, 'Are you here to photograph the sites or the wildlife?'

Dwayne replied, 'I am making a compilation of natural beauty spots within our western regions. This is my last stop, to add the beauty of Yosemite will do it, if I get the right photos. My name is Dwayne,' he said, with an eager expression on his rotund face. David stood up and shook his hand and introduced Natasha. Dwayne nodded his head towards her and said, 'Pleased to meet you both. You are Brit's, aren't you?' David nodded, smiling, knowing that their accent was a giveaway.

Whilst talking to Dwayne they had missed the look that passed between Ava and Sophie. David suddenly thought out of politeness that he should include Sophie and Ava in the conversation as they had offered to provide the picnic. He turned to Ava sitting on the bench opposite and made introductions, Dwayne again said 'Hi' to her.

'Are you capable of doing a strenuous hike? It is all uphill to start with?' she said in a flat voice, as she looked him up and down.

'Oh yes, I am used to difficult terrain, although I normally deal with them alone,' he answered, a cheery smile on his face.

'I guess you can join us,' she said. 'I am pretty sure we have enough food.' She stood up and disappeared into their own tent.

'Sit down,' David told Dwayne. 'We are just going to put the right gear on for the hike.'

'You okay Tash?' David asked, inside their tent.

'Yes,' she answered. 'Dwayne appears to be a nice chap.'

However, she still felt uncomfortable with Ava; why, she could not work out. She put on a lemon-coloured shirt which highlighted her hair colour and added green shorts. David changed into denim shorts and a blue T-shirt. Both put their walking shoes on. David packed their rucksack with essentials.

'We are all going to the same beauty spot, and they seem like nice people,' he replied.

Natasha was not completely convinced, but she was sure that David would not let anything happen to her, so she relaxed a little, and brushed her misgivings away. Dwayne had joined the party as well. The five came together and took the trail that would lead them to the falls. Leaving the tented village behind, they took off at a brisk pace, all wanting to beat the strength of the sun that would come later.

★★★

There were many interesting things to view during the hike. Dwayne seemed to have an expert eye to pick out an interesting rock structure covered by flora that could not at first be seen, but when examined closely and magnified by his camera lens, it was quite lovely. The trail was easy going to start with. The walk from the tented community was approximately four and a half miles to the top of the falls. However, as they approached the Sierra Nevada it became an uphill challenge. As each of their party appeared fit and healthy, it should be a breeze, David thought. He was not concerned.

Sophie chatted to Natasha, David and Dwayne, as they walked, telling them she worked in an advertising agency in 'San Fran' as she called it, her ponytail swishing from one side to the other as her long legs dealt with the upward climb. She asked about them, what had brought them to visit Yosemite? David answered her questions, as did Dwayne. Natasha could not rid herself of her uneasy feelings regarding Ava, so she spoke little. Ava did not seem interested in the question-and-answer scenario, which Sophie kept going. She just kept plodding along, as if she was an expedition leader venturing into unknown territory.

At the halfway point, the party stopped to rest, take a drink of water, and to get their breath back. The sun was becoming stronger, the wispy Cirrus clouds about to burn off. Sophie continued chatting as they all rested, preparing for the final uphill slog. Natasha watched Ava and her feeling of unrest was exacerbated. She felt as if Ava had a hidden agenda, and not a pleasant one. It was on the tip of her tongue to ask David if they could return to camp when Sophie spotted a male horned Mule Deer and drew their attention to it. The moment to act was lost as they all froze to watch it. A magnificent beast, it stood about thirty feet above, them calmly looking at them. Dwayne managed to take several photographs. The click of his camera shutter was very muted. For rather a big man he had managed to move around and perch on the rocks like a mountain goat.

His round face was split by a wide smile as he spoke in sotto voce. 'These are going to be good.'

The deer satisfied that danger was not imminent walked leisurely upwards onto a rocky path it knew well, and eventually disappeared.

That amazing experience was nearly destroyed when Ava barked, 'Time to move on or we will never get there!'

They walked upwards again. As they neared the top, the tons of water pushing through the slim rock crevasse, filled with rainbow colours, age old, stopped any conversation. The full height, 2,425 feet, was apparent. Looking downwards it was dizzying. Dwayne was in his element taking pictures, one after another, moving around as safely as he could, to catch each angle as each of his moves provided a different view.

David hugged Natasha, almost shouting he said, 'Look at this, the wonder of it, the wonder of nature.' Natasha hugged him back, smiling at his enthusiasm as she watched him also taking photos for their memory album. She briefly thought that it was odd that neither Sophie nor Ava took any pictures.

The sun having almost hit its zenith began to cause them all to perspire; but as they had set off early to see the magnificence of Angel Falls, the hike was now downwards and would get easier with every step. While walking to an area where they could speak, and after a short discussion led by Sophie, the party agreed to take the trail that followed the water which landed in a deep pool below, leading to the icy water of Mirror Lake downstream. It was an area of wonderful natural beauty, edged by an ancient Sequoia Forest, the age and the size of the trees was simply stunning.

Sophie smiling and relaxed suggested that they have lunch at Mirror Lake and eat what she had prepared for the outing. Again, Natasha was unsure, but it seemed churlish not to accept the offer as Sophie, she knew, had prepared the picnic. David nodded. Dwayne thanked Sophie. Holding Natasha's hand, David gave her a swift kiss and thought all was well. He hoped that she was relaxing a bit more. They all walked downwards on the trail to Mirror lake.

The magnitude of what they had experienced still could not shift Natasha's unease. It pricked at her. She didn't want to cause David to worry. He was at her side, and there was no real reason she could put her finger on. Dwayne was happily chatting to David, discussing the experience they had had so far that day, happy with the photographs he had been able to capture, and stating that he thought he had the last few to finish his book. Natasha repeatedly reminded herself that it was a lovely day, in a glorious place, one she would probably not be able to come back to and see again in her lifetime. Inwardly, she tried harder to relax. Sophie had stopped commanding ownership of any conversation, which was a relief and Ava continued to march forward as the supposed team leader.

They arrived at Mirror Lake, with the half dome in the background, creating another wonderful backdrop to view.

'I can get a good picture of this too, the light is good,' Dwayne said.

A family with two children sat at one end, the children shrieking as they dipped their toes into the freezing water, their parents laughing at their antics. One of them was the young blonde-haired boy who David had met briefly at the edge of the river near the tented village that morning. The child spotting him, waved briefly.

At the side of the rocky basin where Mirror Lake lay was the Sequoia Forest; the breadth of the trunks were astonishing.

'If I could hollow it out do you think our car would fit through the space?' David asked Natasha. 'These special trees seem to grow so high as if to touch the sky, their age hundreds of years, I would say, at a wild guess.'

Both David and Natasha were stunned at the breadth and height of the trees. Although they had seen photos in books, it was a completely different experience to stand amongst them. Natasha took a deep breath, slowly letting it out as she looked at David, her eyes alight. He squeezed her hand in acknowledgement.

'Some of these trees have trunks wide enough for a car to drive through,' Sophie stated.

'Yes, we know, we did some research,' David responded.

Dwayne said, 'Too good to miss, might not be suitable for my book but I could frame the pictures for me to keep.' He walked around, creating angles that satisfied his photographer's eye.

Ava became impatient, which was obviously her 'norm', stated, 'This is the best spot to have our picnic in, come on.' It led into a small clearing at the edge of the forest.

Sophie tried to soften the command. 'Yes, we should all relax, we should eat, I'm hungry after all the exertion. Aren't you guys?'

Dwayne was the last to force himself away from the imaginary pictures sitting in his brain. They sat down on the rough, dry forest floor. Sophie opened her rucksack and brought food out. Tasty tuna and mayo sandwiches to eat with a fresh salad from a large plastic container. She had brought small plastic plates and plastic forks for the salad. She offered the sandwiches and salad around, smiling. Everyone accepted the food.

But Natasha thought a bit peevishly, "Does she ever stop smiling? She's just too good to be true?" Then she decided she was being grumpy for no substantive reason.

Sophie again dominated the conversation, talking about a brief trip they had taken to Death Valley, how amazing it had been, flicking her ponytail from side to side, a gesture that she appeared to be used to doing. Ava said little again. After the sandwiches and the salad, Sophie dug a small container out from her rucksack that proved to contain small cakes.

'I made these cakes before we left our home. I think they are still fresh, please have one.'

Dwayne, David and Natasha took one, not wanting to appear ungrateful. Ava shook her head and Sophie did not take one either. The family who had been at Mirror Lake when they had arrived, were leaving, and the young boy raised his hand to David, in acknowledgement again. At that time there was another group of people on the other side of Mirror Lake's rocky shoreline.

Within a minute or two Natasha began to feel lightheaded, and when she looked at David he also looked a bit woozy. She drank some cold water offering some to David and Dwayne.

Ava said, 'The heat is getting to me, shall we move nearer to the forest? We can relax in the shade for half an hour before we start our journey back.'

'Yes,' Natasha replied. She thought it must be the heat that made her feel rather strange, plus possibly the exertion of the hike to the top of Angel Falls.

Gathering their belongings, stumbling a little, David helped Natasha to the edge of the forest, followed by Dwayne, Sophie and Ava. They all sat down under the cooling canopy of the trees. Natasha leaned her back against the nearest massive trunk of a towering Sequoia, wondering why she could not focus properly?

'Are you okay?' Sophie, asked her. 'Have another cake. The hike was a little tiring, perhaps you need sugar?'

Natasha waved the offer off, as David did. 'No thank you,' she replied. She felt very strange. Her focus was going in and out. 'David hold my hand,' she whispered. Dwayne accepted a second cake, thanking Sophie again, his speech also a little slurred.

What Natasha, David and Dwayne did not know was that the cakes contained a strong tasteless sedative. Sophie sat crossed legged, her back to Mirror Lake shielding her face from inquisitive eyes; her apparently endless smile on her face. Ava also sat with her back to Mirror Lake next to Sophie. Sophie felt that the drug would be strong enough for what lay ahead, so she was not worried. Ava took a hunting knife out of her rucksack and started to whittle on a fallen branch found on the ground, not paying them any attention. She knew what would happen as she quietly concealed her mounting excitement, waiting for the right moment.

She had wanted Sophie to make them all eat two cakes, but she thought perhaps the fact that the lovesick couple had not would prolong the game. Dwayne would be the easiest target to go for first, he would not be a problem as he was already having trouble staying upright. Surreptitiously she looked at Natasha and David, their eyes wandering around aimlessly, their speech almost gone.

"Their fight against the drug will be stronger," she thought. When they ran, adrenaline would take over for a short time, but that would not stop her. Ava was confident that she would be able to dispose of them all.

Even with the arrival of more people at Mirror Lake, interested in taking photographs and testing the icy temperature of the water as the sun beat down on them.

"This won't be a big problem," Ava thought.

It heightened the thrill so much that her loins warmed. Sophie was good at having a one-sided conversation, laughing now and then, swishing her ponytail. To an onlooker they were five people sitting in the shade, relaxing, nothing outwardly untoward.

She and Sophie had done this so many times. Each location chosen carefully. Ava preferred a wooded environment because the quarry always thought that they could hide behind trees, dodge between them, fleeing for their lives, although they were hampered by being drugged. They had previously murdered three stupid French tourists in Death Valley, pulled them into their web. The expanse of the Salt Flats shielded by a high limestone and sandstone rock structure which presented many caves and natural passages had not saved them. She let her memory roam backwards.

Those three women had run as best they could. The strongest of them had tried to find a cave to hide in, a passage which would be the right one, until she was finally cornered. The other two were easy to deal with. Thinking back on that hunt, she remembered the blood spilt by her hand onto the rocky floor, the sweet smell of it and the colour as it seeped out of each of them. Her anticipation heightened. She also thought about other past kills; the look of utmost fear when she closed in and they were seconds away from death.

A cruel smile twitched on her small mouth, the warmth grew and grew inside her. She could hardly stop herself from wriggling. She was ready to start this hunt. Ava thought it might be an easy one, but she knew how to extend the time to the maximum, for her own pleasure. Sophie had already wiped the utensils they had brought with an antiseptic cleaner. No fingerprints would be left behind, just an abandoned rucksack, without a label, containing untraceable bits and pieces. Sophie would ensure that the plastic water bottles were removed, as well as any other incriminating articles.

Looking at Sophie, Ava hissed, 'Make them run now, make them run. I am ready.' Ava's dull brown eyes were lit up by an unnatural glint.

Sophie standing took a small calibre gun out of her rucksack and with no smile on her face she waved it at the group in front of her and said, 'Get up and run into the forest, all of you! It is your only hope. Do it now!'

Befuddled reality came to David as he looked at the unsmiling face of Sophie with the gun in her hand, and the knife in Ava's as she stood beside her. The threatening stance they both had, blocked the route to Mirror Lake. Dwayne looked up too and he realised that something was very wrong, although he was very confused.

'Get up, man! You must run now,' David said. He grabbed Dwayne's arm and forced him to stand up.

His mind whirled. Drugged as he was, he asked himself how he had missed the danger signs? There was no time for an answer. He pulled Natasha up, still slumped against the tree.

'Tash, Tash, we have to run!' he said. 'No matter what, we must run. Don't let go of my hand, run now.'

Ava watched the three of them trying to run as fast as they could, staggering along a path leading deeper into the forest. Fat Dwayne was trying his best to keep up, his precious camera still over his shoulder, swinging from side to side. She took out a cigarette and lit it. She only ever smoked at the beginning of a hunt. In her warped mind, the five minutes it took her to smoke it gave her prey some time to escape, and the false hope that they needed, which titillated her imagination even more as she wondered how it must feel to be hunted.

Above them the trees whispered as a slight breeze ruffled their foliage. No sun dappled the ground they stumbled over; they were lost in a greyish world. David tried to force his legs to be stronger, and confused as he was, he realised that some form of drug had been given to them.

"Come on man, come on. Think! Think!" he repeated over and over in his brain, dragging Natasha along with him. He could see small, barely distinguishable paths through the Sequoias that one could just follow. Instinct kicked in. "Don't follow the paths," he thought. "Go somewhere else." He knew that Natasha was crying as he pulled her along, but she had not let go of his hand.

'Come on darling,' he rasped at her, moving diagonally through the forest, swerving off the path.

Shouting backward, he told Dwayne not to follow a path, but rather to go in a different direction. He could see him struggling to run, behind him, but his responsibility was Natasha. He could not look after two people, although he wanted to. She was far more important to him. Reluctantly, he focused on her and tried to work out how to save both of them.

He shouted again, 'Get off the path Dwayne, now!'

Almost dragging her David kept changing direction until they were only surrounded by trees, with no path in sight, no sound, other than the slight breeze rustling through the leaves high above them. They had left Dwayne behind. He could not see or hear Ava and Sophie. He thought that they might have a chance, although he was completely lost.

'I can't go any further,' Natasha gasped. 'I have to rest for a minute or two.'

David looked wildly around for a safe place. Perhaps the drug was wearing off slowly with the exercise or from the adrenaline that had fuelled his flight. In front of him was a massive Sequoia tree with a natural hollow inside, at ground level, big enough for them both to shelter in. It looked like a little hut.

'Here,' David said, 'five minutes of rest.' They sat with their arms around each other almost hidden from sight. In a hushed voice David spoke into Natasha's ear. 'We must move on, we are not safe here, we have to get deeper into the forest. Our only hope is to try and stay hidden until nightfall.'

'Where is Dwayne?' Natasha whispered.

David shook his head and put his finger to her lips to stop her from talking. Natasha nodded her head, tears welling up in her eyes. They quietly moved on again after a short rest.

★★★

After half an hour of fruitless searching Ava snarled at Sophie. In a low voice she said, 'You stupid bitch, how many times do I have to tell you how to drug them and how to watch where they go, swishing your stupid ponytail. Which fucking way have they gone?' A slight movement came into her peripheral vision, the soft sound of heavy breathing. 'Quiet,' she hissed at Sophie.

Softly she walked towards the slight noise, the shift of a foot, blocking out the sound of leaves rustling above her. Signing Sophie to follow. She had noticed the precious camera, with the large lens dropped about twenty feet away from where she thought he was. She approached from the back of the wide trunk, her tread like that of a cat. She was in front of him before he even heard her.

Dwayne, snot running out of his nose, feral panic in his eyes, stood with his back pressed against the rough bark of the towering tree. Gulping, his eyes taking in both Sophie, gun in hand and Ava waving her knife under his nose he said, 'Why, Why?'

'Why not?' Ava answered. 'I haven't got time to talk to you, I have others to find. Don't waste your breath as it is the last one you will have.'

It happened so fast that Dwayne did not see it coming. As he tried to open his mouth to speak, his windpipe was destroyed, his neck slashed.

Ava quickly stepped back to admire her handywork. The heat heightened in her groin as she watched blood pumping and splashing over his shirt, some of the peripheral spots freckling the tree behind him. She waited for his body to react, sniffing that wonderful smell, drawing it into her nostrils deeply. Before Dwayne's legs gave in and he slowly slid to the ground, she noticed that he had peed himself. There was a large wet stain on his knee length shorts, and a few distinguishable drops on his boots. That weakness made her almost want to scream with satisfaction. She inhaled again. She was sure she could distinguish that scent from the blood dripping onto the ground.

Sophie watched Ava as she panted, and she knew that she had come to her first climax. Quietly Sophie said, 'We should move on, find the other two.'

'Yes,' Ava, replied. Physically shaking herself, she cleaned the knife hilt on a piece of the fabric of Dwayne's shirt. 'I think the other one with his prissy girl will not be too difficult to find. I want to gut the girl first, while he watches me do that,' Ava said. 'Use your skills, find their fucking trail before they get too deep in.'

Ava was at the height of her kill urge. Blood pumped fast around her body. She was on fire. She needed to sate the urge to see more blood, find the prey, and have another climax.

They retraced their steps and Sophie studied the ground intently. Ava continued after a short time to swear and mumble as they jogged through the forest, looking for a trace of where Natasha and David might have gone, or were hiding. Sophie tried to find anything that could indicate in which direction they could have gone. She found the hut at the base of the huge Sequoia, but it was difficult to follow their tracks from there. She was sure that they were still in the forest, although the drug may have worn off a little.

"They are not that clever," she thought. They would still be disoriented. The hunt was still on. Patience was needed sometimes to get your kill. However, she knew that Ava had little patience when the urge to destroy was upon her.

Searching for any evidence that the forest floor gave, there was no clue. Listening to Ava cursing behind her, talking to herself, Sophie felt a coldness which warned of anger building within herself. She had learnt to suppress it many times before. She was the lure, the one who set up each kill, the one who people warmed to. Most people disliked Ava on sight. She was the charmer who got everything into place so that Ava with her lust to kill could do as she wished. As Ava's lover for the last five years, at the beginning she had done anything to make Ava as happy as she could, but her constant mean spirit was becoming exceptionally hard for her to deal with.

She had created each hunt for Ava, she had done the research, choosing each spot, finding the quickest way to leave, and cleaning up so no fingerprints were left behind; no evidence that could link them to a death. Ava had killed nineteen people up to that day. After each hunt, Ava became gentle and caring towards her, briefly, but the time between the kills had shortened drastically. Now Ava quickly became spiteful and petulant. She hardly had a kind word to speak to Sophie, until the next hunt was set up, which always took time to plan. There were few kind words or gentle caresses nowadays. Trudging through the Sequoia Forest looking for tracks, so Ava could use her knife again. Sophie's anger boiled up more, and she began to feel totally disrespected.

Pushing past Sophie, Ava stomped forward. 'This is bloody stupid, find them, do your job. What is the point of having you in my life if you can't get me what I need?' Ava spoke, not turning around to look at Sophie, not observing the fact that Sophie's light grey eyes had turned the colour of flint; not seeing that her smile had disappeared, and that she was clenching her teeth, causing white flesh to appear around her lips.

Today, Ava's endless impatience and frankly rather scary blood lust had opened the door to the complete viciousness of the squat woman who tramped forward, her back to her lover. Sophie suddenly felt it like a heavy weight on her shoulders.

"One more unkind word from her," Sophie thought, trying to control her temper. She wondered why she had fallen in love with Ava? At the beginning it had been extraordinarily exciting, their lovemaking after each event when they were safely home, had been sadistically passionate, reckless; it had turned Sophie on. But now ...?

Ava turned on her heel and facing Sophie she said, 'God woman, why are you standing there doing nothing? How long do I have to wait? Get your arse into gear, they are out there, go and fucking find them.'

'Perhaps a drink of water may help you feel a little better, before we move on,' Sophie replied.

Ava missed the look of murder in her partner's eyes as Sophie had forced herself to put her usual warm smile on her face.

'Yes, give me some water, for God's sake do something useful.'

Sophie did as she was told, but instead of taking the bottle of water from her rucksack she brought out the gun and without flinching, she shot Ava in the forehead. The balance had shifted. Ava's reckless needs had become too much to deal with. Before Ava fell to the ground a look of surprise settled on her face.

The sound resonated around the forest. Birds flew out of the extraordinary tall trees. David trying to urge Natasha to run deeper into the forest to find some sort of refuge, stopped in his tracks. Natasha flinched, looking wildly around, not knowing what had happened, although the sound seemed not to be too near them. It was certainly a gun shot. David threw his arms around Natasha. The action of protecting, shielding her, was instinctive. He then pulled her behind the nearest huge Sequoia tree. No other sound followed.

'We have to stay where we are,' David whispered. 'It is not safe to move right now.' Natasha her eyes huge, just nodded, her body shivering as she clung onto him.

Sophie looked at Ava's body lying on the ground before her with a strange expression on her face; one she had never seen when Ava had been alive. She thought her deceased partner looked even smaller than when she had been standing. She had no feelings for the bully who had taken over her life years before. She calmly checked for any identification carried by Ava, clothing tags, and any pockets not cleaned of scraps of paper. She placed the gun and the knife into her rucksack, thinking that they would be easy to ditch. She turned around to retrace her steps, and walked towards Mirror Lake. It would not take her long to find it. She would pack up their scant belongings in tent number whatever it was, and leave Yosemite before nightfall, with no trace left behind. That was something that she was good at doing.

Sophie did not care about the prey, they would find their own way out eventually. They had been extremely lucky, she would be far away by then. She was not worried about David or Natasha giving details about her or Ava to the police or to the rangers, should they choose to report the event. Everything she had told them had been false, including the names 'Sophie' and 'Ava' and therefore untraceable. Who knew when the corpse of the chubby chap would be found?

★★★

As Julia walked towards the tented village, she thought about changing her hair, cutting it short. She had liked the auburn colour of Natasha's, but she decided on chocolate brown. Having made that decision, vain as it was, she then thought she might move to the Deep South, reinventing herself again. Sophie had died with Ava. Her normal smile on her face, swishing her ponytail from side to side, she felt sure that she would find another lover, a kinder one, she hoped. A spring came to her step as she quickened her pace, her long legs striding out, as she began to plan the rest of her future.

★★★

As the long silence continued after the gun shot, the drug having left his body, David had a feeling that they could cautiously move. He had lost his bearings as they had run this way and that, but he had to find a way out.

'Tash, we need to try and get back to safety. Do you trust me to do that?' he asked.

'I do of course, I do, get me out, get me home David.' He nodded. It was not going to be easy, he steeled his back, and safety beckoned.

'This way,' David told Natasha, his sense of direction kicking in.

Wandering around they came across the body of Ava. 'Oh God! No! No! Can it get any worse?' Natasha whimpered.

'Don't look,' David said as he pulled her away from the body, noting that Ava had been shot in the head.

Natasha was crying, shivering. All he could think to do was to hold her tight and kiss her face, kiss her tears away, whisper loving words into her ear, calm her down. It was his job to get them out of this forest alive.

Natasha pulled herself together slowly. Her dirty face streaked with tears, she said again, 'Get me out of this bloody forest David, please. I cannot take much more.'

'I promise you I will find a way out,' was his reply.

They walked forward, he picked up a faint path which he felt was a good sign. David searched to find the Sierra Nevada mountains, a guide that he was on the right path, and that they were moving in the right direction. He thought back to Natasha's reluctance to walk the trail with Ava and Sophie.

"Listen to her instincts more," he told himself. However, now he must get her to safety, and find Mirror Lake. Once there, it would be easy.

Natasha was exhausted, but he encouraged every step she made. As the forest thinned the Sierra Nevada appeared in his sight above the treetops. He could not stop a laugh from sheer relief.

'What? What?' Natasha asked. Her head had been down watching each step she made.

'We are nearly there, Tash. Keep going my love, keep going.' In what was a short time, compared to what they had endured, they came to the clearing where their awful experience had started. An abandoned rucksack lay on the ground, Mirror Lake was in front of them.

Natasha stood and looked at Mirror Lake. Her mind rushed back to how they had started their day, so happily, planning an adventure to remember. Now she wanted to forget this day had ever happened.

'I am thirsty, can I drink this water?' she asked David.

'Yes, it is clean mountain water. Drink and splash some on your face, it will help to revive you. I am sure it is less than half an hour's downhill walk to the tented village.'

***

They walked into the village as evening darkened the sky. A vivid orange sunset sent vibrant streaks of colour through it. Families were preparing to cook, men enjoying a beer as they waited for charcoal to heat, women making salad or washing potatoes to bake, a glass of wine on the table, children running around happy as they had done in the morning, playing. All was normal and natural. Nobody took too much notice of them. Nervously they approached tent 39. The tent opposite them was empty, the flaps open, no evidence left that it had been occupied earlier that day.

'What do we do?' Natasha asked David as she slumped down on the bench outside their tent, too tired to walk inside, uncaring about how she may look.

She felt that if she lay down on the bed that she would never get up again. David opened a bottle of chilled wine from the fridge. Putting a glass in front of them both, he filled them to the brink. He noticed that there was a slight tremor in his hand.

'Drink this first, then go and have a shower, it will make you feel better. I do not know why that works, but I think it will strengthen your resolve. Then I will cook some food and we will talk about our next move.'

Her beautiful eyes brimmed with tears as she looked at him, her auburn hair looked like a haystack. Her clothes were filthy, like his. Even the wash at Mirror Lake had not removed what the day had done to them.

"God, I love this woman," he thought. "I am so lucky".

Natasha nodded, drank her wine, and when a little more strength had returned, she went for a shower. David put charcoal on the BBQ and started to coax it to heat.

He poured another glass of wine for himself, downing it quickly. He poured another one and one for Tash to return to. He was thinking about Dwayne.

Returning to David she looked a little stronger, she went into the tent and came out wearing a flowing multi coloured kaftan.

'Right my turn now,' David said. 'I won't be long, you are safe, try to relax and drink your wine.'

During David's absence Natasha looked around her at the normality, a holiday situation, thinking about how every person she looked at didn't know anything about how she felt, or what had occurred and how a few hours could change a life.

She watched cheeky children run up and down the path, happily. A young mother passed holding a baby in her arms in a blue baby grow suit. She was rocking it, whispering to the child, trying to settle it for a night's sleep. The baby was waving its arm, its hand trying to touch the face of his mother, or clasp some of her hair.

"Wonderful, all so very normal," she thought again.

David returned and put a tracksuit on. Although the evening was not cold; he felt a chill from inside his body. The charcoal was ready, and he threw thick hamburgers onto the BBQ, buttered baps, cut up tomatoes, found some salad and put mustard on the table.

'David, I have to do something,' she told him.

'Now?' he asked, about to put food on their plates.

'Yes, now,' Natasha replied. Stating that she went into their tent and gathered up every piece of clothing they had both worn that day. 'Get rid of it! Get rid of it now! Throw all of it in a bin.' He did as she asked. He understood what that gesture meant.

As evening turned to nightfall, the streaks of the dropping sun disappeared.

After eating, David opened a second bottle of wine and Natasha asked again, in a low voice, 'What should we do?'

He answered in as strong a voice as he could muster, he had been thinking it through. 'First, I doubt that very few people took any notice of those two women in the tent opposite ours, which is now empty. It is a busy place, at the height of the season, nobody looks hard at the people around them, it is a holiday environment. If I walked up to anybody and asked them to describe you, I doubt I could find one who could. Second, for whatever reason we agreed to go to Angel Falls with them. It was probably my fault. Dwayne asked to join the party, he told us he had come for one day, therefore he cannot be traced to any room.'

'But where is Dwayne?' Natasha interrupted.

'I don't know, darling,' he responded. 'Perhaps safely driving to his home.' David wanted to keep his train of thought on course. 'Third, when we arrived at Mirror Lake, unsuspecting we were all drugged, the cake, I guess. Being in that state, if we were questioned about the experience there would be little belief of how we say things transpired. How we had to flee for our lives. How we managed to hide from them and then how we escaped to arrive back here.'

'But what about the body of Ava, shot, that still lies in that forest? Do you think Dwayne is safe, alive?' Natasha asked. 'We must go to the police and report what happened.'

'No, my love, no. We had to run away, deep into the forest which was empty except for the three of us trying to hide. We went one way, Dwayne took another. He ate two cakes so probably he was affected by the drug more than we were. I don't know what happened to him. Ava and Sophie were stalking us.

The only person that could have shot Ava was her co-conspirator, Sophie. She pulled a gun on us, pointed it at us and told us all to run. Ava had a knife. Ava is dead, killed by Sophie for whatever reason. Perhaps she got what was coming to her, ghastly as that is. No, we will leave this place tomorrow. In time we will forget this. Will you marry me, please?'

'But ...' Natasha said.

'Please, no more buts, is your answer yes or no?'

David watched the weariness appear to lift from her face, the lines smoothed out around her blue eyes. Natasha realised that no matter how difficult it was, she had to shake off the horror of this day. Neither of them had all the answers, but they had survived. She examined her lover, the man who had saved her life, protected her, encouraged her not to give in, the man she adored, whom she wanted to spend the rest of her life with.

Squeezing him tightly she said, 'Oh, yes, yes, yes, yes.'

'Good, now come to bed, I want to touch every part of your body, until I have no energy left or you tell me to stop. We will go to sleep. We have an early start tomorrow.'

Natasha unbelievably quickly felt very amorous. She looked at his thick blond hair, his wonderful kind, caring odd eyes, his body, she needed her man inside her. She wanted to feel his hands on her, running over her body. She wanted to wrap her arms and legs around him pretending in her imagination that she was a limpet, unable to be shaken off. She wanted so very much the way that he brought her to the point of no return, watching her in that second, before joining her. She followed him into tent 39.

★★★

As dawn came, David woke Natasha. 'Come with me, we have to leave here with a special memory. I think I can find one.'

Looking quizzically at him she threw her kaftan on, not bothering to brush her tangled hair after their night of passion. David quickly donned his tracksuit and led her through the tents, the odd one open, a person standing outside stretching ready to meet the new day, who they waved at. He guided her down the path, through the fir forest, stopping before the small meadow where they had made love. The sound of the Merced River rushing by broke the silence that surrounded them. David put his finger to his lips and pointed. In front of Natasha stood a small blonde-haired boy, wearing a green T-shirt and black shorts. He was barefoot. Ten yards away from him stood a doe Mule Deer, at the river's edge. They were both looking at each other fascinated.

Silence, seemed to descend, and the sound of the river diminished. The seconds that passed were palpable, the stillness of the tableaux in front of her brought tears to her eyes, but they were tears of happiness and amazement. The rising sun, as it usually did, bathed the space between the boy and the Mule Deer in stunning, shimmering gold. The doe took one last look at the boy then bounded into the forest.

The boy turned and walking past them he said in a matter-of-fact tone to David, 'I told you, she is always here.'

'How amazingly wonderful,' Natasha said.

'Yes,' David agreed, delighted at the look on her face. The strain of the previous day had almost disappeared. 'Now come on we have to get out of here quickly. When can you marry me?'

'Tomorrow, would not be too soon,' Natasha replied, her whole face alight with happiness. Holding his hand very tightly, she walked by his side back to tent 39.

On the return walk through the tented village she noticed the young mother whispering to her baby, gently lifting him up to bring a smile to his face, a gurgle of happiness.

She thought, "One day I will do that." She remembered that David had asked her if she would like to have children, although that moment now seemed lightyears before.

They showered, dressed and packed quickly. Once in their hired car they left Yosemite National Park behind. Neither looked back. They got married three months later.

★★★

The body of Ava was found the next day by a park ranger checking the Mirror Lake area. Even though her cause of death was classed as a possible murder, all investigations and enquiries did not reveal anything that could be followed through or prove her identity. Months later she was buried under the name of Jane Doe. The body of Dwayne, sadly, was not found for several weeks, mutilated by scavengers, wolves, foxes or bears. The cause of death was difficult to establish due to the actions of the animals, as was identification. A hiker discovered a rather expensive looking camera, in the forest, covered by foliage. He liked to walk away from paths that were well trodden. He diligently handed it in to the rangers who dealt with lost and found.

The camera was never claimed, the photographic roll when developed held no clues either as each negative was of a natural formation within the park. A connection between the two deaths was not made either. Neither had been reported missing. Yosemite contained hundreds of lodge rooms, and cabins of all sizes, including the accommodation in the tented village, not to mention, in the height of the season, the hundreds of day trippers who visited the area. Yosemite National Park covered a vast area, 748,542 acres, some parts easily accessible, others not so much. Mysterious things happened on the odd occasion. The park rangers were always kept quite busy.

★★★

Julia, aka Zoe sat in a jazz club in the French Quarter, New Orleans, drinking a very cold beer from the bottle. She wore a figure hugging short red dress. Long silver earrings almost brushed her shoulders. Her athletic legs were stretched out in front of her, silver coloured flip flops on her feet. She had learned how to swish her new shorter brown hair. Her smile remained the same as she looked at her new lover singing soulful music on the small stage in front of her. She found it easy to brush annoying, bothersome memories out of her mind.

Enjoying the sultry glances from the woman on the stage she thought, "Life is not that bad," as she swatted a mosquito away from her face.

★★★

HERZ FÜR AUTOREN A HEART FOR AUTHORS À L'ÉCOUTE DES AUTEURS MIA KAPΔIA ΓΙΑ ΣΥΓΓΡ
ΑΡΤΑ FÖR FÖRFATTARE UN CORAZÓN POR LOS AUTORES YAZARLARIMIZA GÖNÜL VERELIM SZÍ
ORE PER AUTORI ET HJERTE FOR FORFATTERE EEN HART VOOR SCHRIJVERS TEMOS OS AUTO
ZÖINKÉRT SERCE DLA AUTORÓW EIN HERZ FÜR AUTOREN A HEART FOR AUTHORS À L'ÉCOU
ORAÇÃO ВСЕЙ ДУШОЙ К АВТОРАМ ETT HJÄRTA FÖR FÖRFATTARE À LA ESCUCHA DE LOS AUTOF
AUTEURS MIA KAPΔIA ΓΙΑ ΣΥΓΓΡΑΦΕΙΣ UN CUORE PER AUTORI ET HJERTE FOR FORFATTERE EEN F
ARIMIZA GÖ RE ZÖINKÉRT SERCE DLA AUTORÓW EIN HERZ FÜF
VOOR SCHRIJVERS S O ÇÃO ВСЕЙ ДУШОЙ К АВТОРАМ ETT HJÄRTA FÖF

The author

Faye Starling was born in Southport, UK. At the
age of ten, she left the UK with her parents to go
to Kenya, where she completed her education.
Faye was educated to secondary level after which
she attended secretarial college.
Faye lived in Uganda and Tanzania until she got
married at 18. She and her husband lived in Bang-
ladesh and Ghana. After her divorce she returned
to the UK with her son and joined the police at
24. She spent some time as a teacher at a secretarial college before she remarried in 1977 and
moved to Hong Kong in 1983. There she became
a director of an English training company. In 1997
Faye moved to Cyprus and lived there until 2004.
Moving to Morocco, she bought land and became
the project manager of her self-designed home.
She returned to the UK in 2019.
Her favourite activities are animal care, gardening,
cooking and writing. She has written a children's
book containing 4 short stories awaiting publica-
tion this year.

The publisher

*He who stops
getting better
stops being good.*

This is the motto of novum publishing, and our focus
is on finding new manuscripts, publishing them and
offering long-term support to the authors.
Our publishing house was founded in 1997, and since
then it has become THE expert for new authors and
has won numerous awards.

**Our editorial team will peruse each manuscript
within a few weeks free of charge and without
obligation.**

You will find more information about
novum publishing and our books on the internet:

w w w . n o v u m - p u b l i s h i n g . c o . u k